If I Had a Snowplow

By **Jean L. S. Patrick** • Illustrated by **Karen Dugan**

Boyds Mills Press

Text copyright © 2001 by Jean Patrick
Illustrations copyright © 2001 by Karen Dugan
All rights reserved

Published by Caroline House
Boyds Mills Press, Inc.
A Highlights Company
815 Church Street
Honesdale, Pennsylvania 18431
Printed in China

U.S. Cataloging-in-Publication Data
(Library of Congress Standards)

Patrick, Jean.
If I had a snowplow / by Jean Patrick ; illustrated by Dugan,
Karen.—1st ed.
[32]p. : col. Ill. ; cm.
Summary: While snowbound in their rural home, a son
shares with his mother all the helpful things he would do—just for her.
ISBN 1-56397-746-X
1. Mothers and sons — Fiction. 2. Children — Fiction. I. Dugan, Karen,
ill. II. Title.
[E] 21 2001 AC CIP
00-103741

First edition, 2001
The text of this book is set in 17-point Usherwood Book.

10 9 8 7 6 5 4 3 2

For Catherine, Shea, and Kendall
—J. L. S. P.

For Kyle Robert Fairbanks, and all who made him possible: Marguerite and
William Davis, Judith and Robert Davis, Lesley, Donald and older brother
D. J. Fairbanks, all his great-aunts and uncles, aunts and uncles,
assorted cousins, and last but not least, the great Bianca, and
great-in-training Sabrina.

With love,
—K. D.

If I had a snowplow, you know what I'd do?

I'd crash through the deep snow, just for you.

I'd clear a new road,

a smooth road,

a let's-get-through road.

I'd crash through the deep snow, just for you.

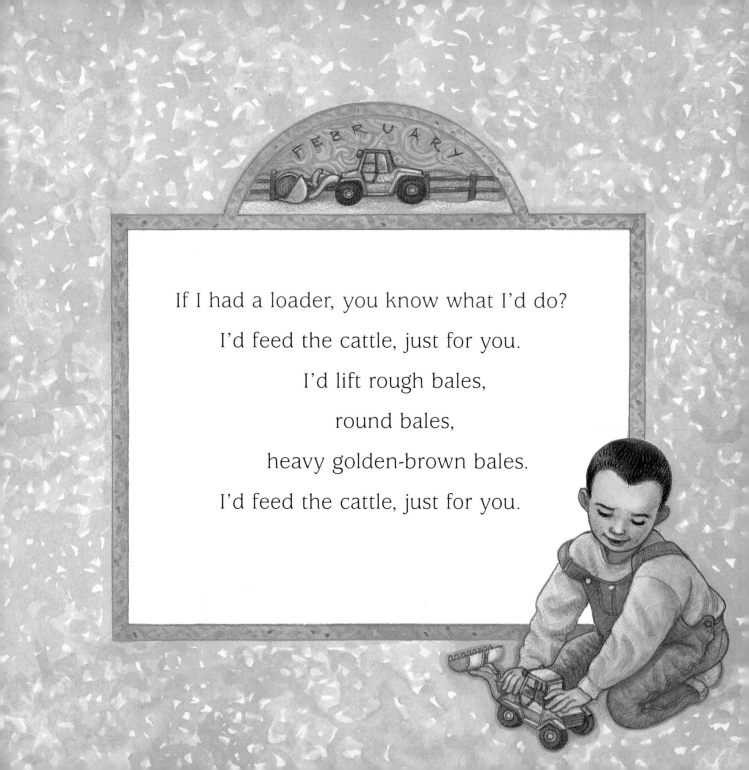

FEBRUARY

If I had a loader, you know what I'd do?

I'd feed the cattle, just for you.

I'd lift rough bales,

round bales,

heavy golden-brown bales.

I'd feed the cattle, just for you.

If I had a cement mixer, you know what I'd do?

I'd pour a sidewalk, just for you.

I'd pave a dry walk,

a wide walk,

a your-hand-in-mine walk.

I'd pour a sidewalk, just for you.

If I had a tractor, you know what I'd do?

I'd disk the garden, just for you.

I'd till the flat dirt,

the firm dirt,

the cool, black-worm dirt.

I'd disk the garden, just for you.

If I had a tree spade, you know what I'd do?

I'd plant a forest, just for you.

I'd bring you spring trees,

shade trees,

Mother's Day bouquet trees.

I'd plant a forest, just for you.

If I had a tow truck, you know what I'd do?

I'd pull a picnic basket, just for you.

We'd eat tuna salad,

taco salad,

pickle-powered pasta salad.

I'd pull a picnic basket, just for you.

If I had a fire truck, you know what I'd do?

I'd water the garden, just for you.

Then we'd have a spray day,

a play day,

a shouting, soaking heyday.

I'd water the garden, just for you.

If I had a cherry picker, you know what I'd do?

I'd hang the highest hammock, just for you.

We'd swing through the blue sky,

the bright sky,

'til stars fill the night sky.

I'd hang the highest hammock, just for you.

If I had a backhoe, you know what I'd do?

I'd harvest vegetables, just for you.

I'd dig potatoes,

dump potatoes,

lift and load the plump potatoes.

I'd harvest vegetables, just for you.

OCTOBER

If I had a bulldozer, you know what I'd do?

I'd clear the backyard, just for you.

We'd fall in leaves,

crawl in leaves,

tumble through the autumn leaves.

I'd clear the backyard, just for you.

NOVEMBER

If I had a tall crane, you know what I'd do?

I'd gather firewood, just for you.

I'd lift heavy logs,

stumpy logs,

crooked, long, and bumpy logs.

I'd gather firewood, just for you.

If I had a dump truck, you know what I'd do?

I'd haul surprises, just for you.

I'd deliver fat presents,

thin presents,

up-to-your-chin presents.

I'd haul surprises, just for you.

But since I don't have a snowplow,

loader,

cement mixer,

tractor,

tree spade,

tow truck,

fire truck,

cherry picker,

backhoe,

bulldozer,

tall crane, or

dump truck,

you know what I'll do?

I'll stay inside, close to you.

I'll give you huge hugs,

strong hugs,

love-you-all-day-long hugs.

I'll stay inside, close to you.